Over on a Desert

Somewhere in the World

By Marianne Berkes
Illustrated by Jill Dubin
Dawn Publications

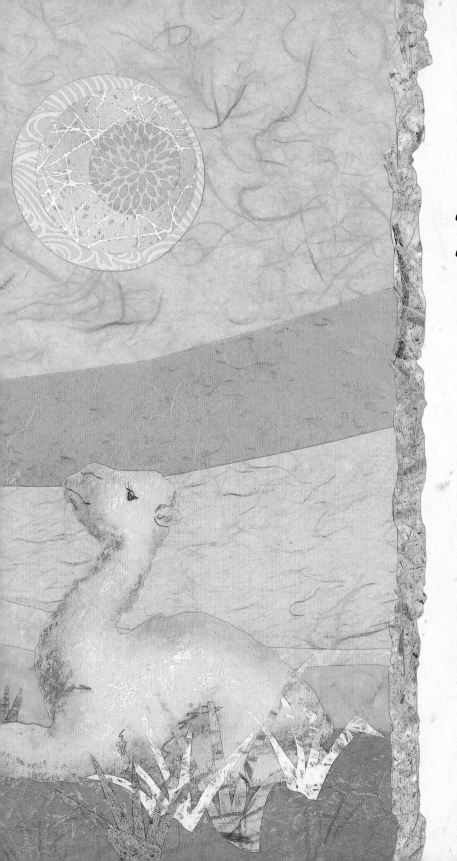

Over on a desert
Resting in the hot sun
Lived a tall mother camel
And her little *calf* one.

"Kneel," said the mother.
"I kneel," said the one.
So they knelt in the desert
Resting in the hot sun.

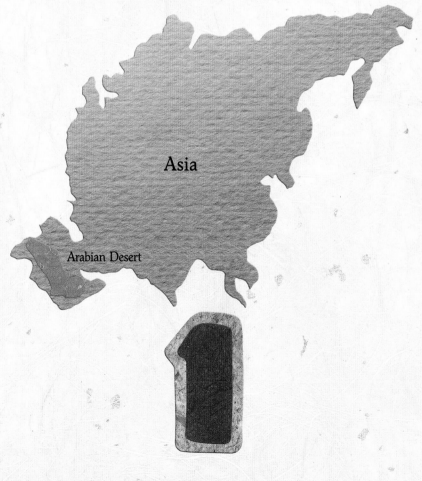

Asia

Arabian Desert

Over on a desert
Where the barrel cactus grew
Lived a mother gila monster
And her little *hatchlings* two.

"Flick," said the mother.
"We flick," said the two.
So they flicked with their tongues
Where the barrel cactus grew.

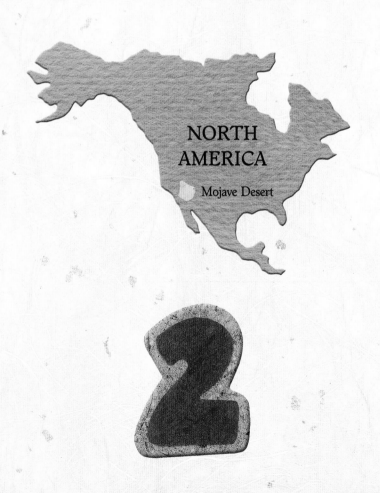

NORTH
AMERICA

Mojave Desert

Over on a desert
Near a camelthorn tree
Lived a slender mother meerkat
And her little *pups* three.

"Stand" said the mother
"We stand," said the three.
So they stood and they watched
Near a camelthorn tree.

AFRICA

Kalahari
Desert

Over on a desert
On a hot, sandy floor
Lived a wild mother dingo
And her little *pups* four.

"Sniff," said the mother.
"We sniff," said the four.
So they sniffed in a pack
On a hot, sandy floor.

Over on a desert
Where mesquite trees thrive
Lived a mother armadillo
And her little *pups* five.

"Dig," said the mother.
"We dig," said the five.
So they dug with their claws
Where mesquite trees thrive.

SOUTH
AMERICA

Monte Desert

Over on a desert
Eating cactus that pricks
Lived a mother javelina
And her little *reds* six.

"Snort," said the mother.
"We snort," said the six.
So they grunted and they snorted
Eating cactus that pricks.

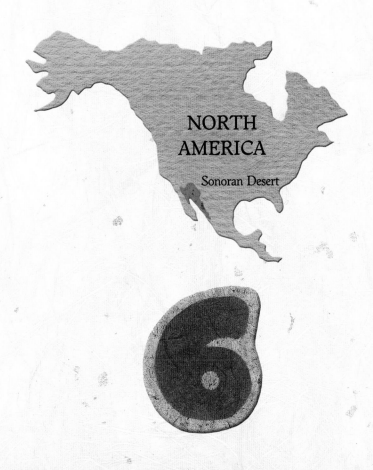

NORTH
AMERICA

Sonoran Desert

Over on a desert
Where saguaros reach to heaven
Lived a mother desert tortoise
And her little *hatchlings* seven.

"Hide," said the mother.
"We hide," said the seven.
So they hid in their shells
Where saguaros reach to heaven.

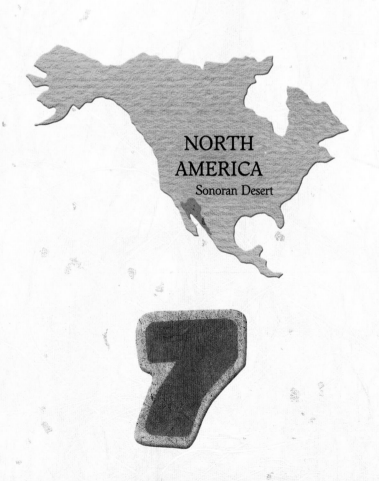

NORTH
AMERICA
Sonoran Desert

7

Over on a desert
Where they often go out late
Lived a shy mother jerboa
And her little *pups* eight.

"Jump," said the mother.
"We jump," said the eight.
So they jumped way up high
Where they often go out late.

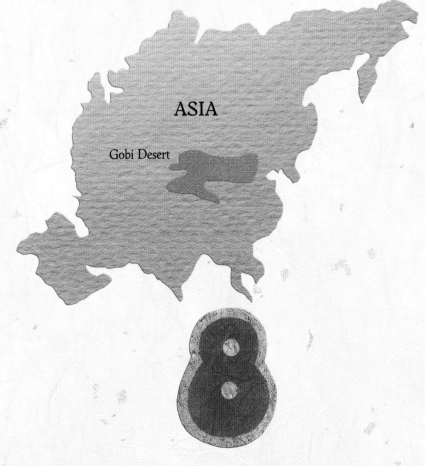

ASIA

Gobi Desert

Over on a desert
In the hot sunshine
Lived a mother roadrunner
And her little *chicks* nine.

"Coo," said the mother.
"We coo," said the nine.
So they cooed as they ran
In the hot sunshine.

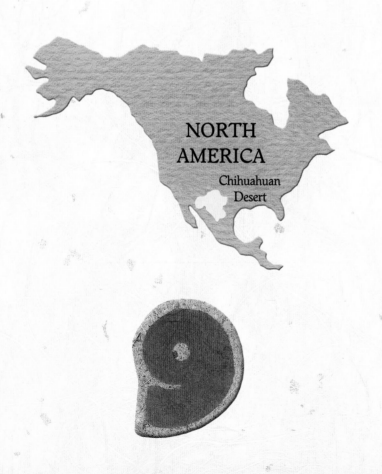

NORTH
AMERICA

Chihuahuan
Desert

Over on a desert
In their underground den
Lived a clever desert fox
And his little *kits* ten.

"Listen," said the father.
"We listen," said the ten.
As they heard the sound of laughing
From their underground den.

Sahara Desert

AFRICA

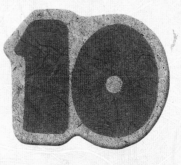

NORTH
AMERICA

Mojave Desert
Sonoran Desert
Chihuahuan
Desert

EUROPE

Arabian
Desert

Sahara Desert

AFRICA

SOUTH
AMERICA

Kalahari
Desert

Monte
Desert

ANTARCTICA
Desert Continent

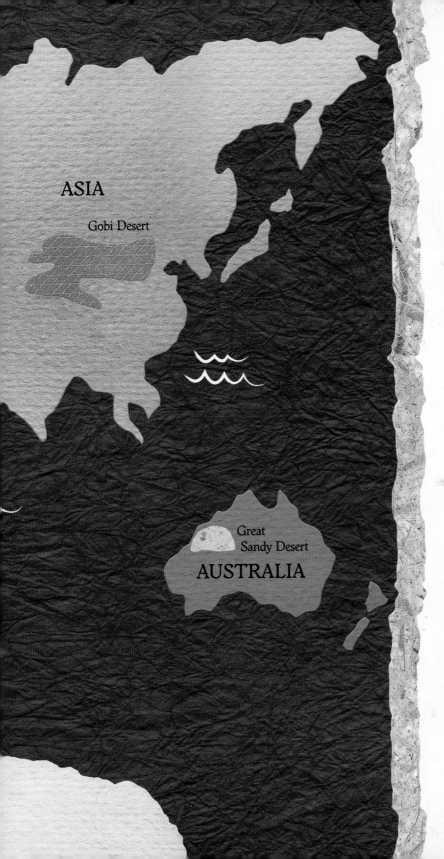

Around the world are deserts.
Some are very far away.
Can you find the different deserts
Where the baby animals play?

Then go back to the beginning
And spy with your eyes
To find the hidden creatures.
Every page has a surprise!

Fact or Fiction?

In this variation of the traditional song, "Over in the Meadow," all the desert animals actually behave as they have been portrayed. Camels *kneel*, armadillos *dig*, and roadrunners *coo*. That's a fact! But do they have the number of babies as in this rhyme? No! That is fiction. Gila monsters lay 3-14 eggs, not two as in this story, and dingoes can have a litter of as many as ten pups. But the author created her story to rhyme, so she combined fact and fiction. Do the animals live on the deserts shown on the map? Yes, they do, and sometimes they live in other places, too.

Baby animals are cared for in different ways by their parents. Usually, it is the mother who takes care of the babies. But both mother and father roadrunners take care of their chicks until they are no longer helpless. And a father fennec fox hunts for food for his kits and remains part of the family. However, male javelinas take no part in raising or protecting their babies. Nature has different ways of ensuring the survival of different species.

Desert Facts

About 20% of the land on Earth is desert. Did you know there are both hot *and* cold deserts? The characteristic *all* deserts have in common is that they are very dry. Deserts receive less than 10 inches (24 mm) of moisture a year. All of the deserts in this book are hot deserts with the exception of the Gobi, a cold desert in Asia. Another cold desert—Antarctica—is shown on the map at the end of the story. It's the largest desert in the world and is covered completely by ice. It receives less precipitation per year than the Sahara, which is the largest hot desert on earth.

Plants that live in this extremely dry habitat have unique adaptations to help them survive. Cacti and succulents have the ability to conserve water. For example, the shallow root system of a saguaro cactus spreads out near the surface of the desert to collect as much water as possible after a rain. And its thick stem stores water for times of drought. The spines on a barrel cactus not only keep animals from eating it, they also prevent water loss by reflecting away sunlight. Wildflower seeds can remain dormant in dry, desert soil for dozens of years. When there is a wet season, they burst into vibrant blooms, as shown by the poppies and lupines on the page with the tortoises.

One of the ways animals have adapted to living in the desert is by minimizing the time they spend in the hot sun. They're nocturnal (active at night) and crepuscular (active at dawn and dusk). Some animals rest in whatever shade they can find during the day, such as under a camelthorn tree on the Kalahari Desert. Other animals dig below the soil to escape intense heat. Some rodents even plug the entrances to their burrows to keep out the hot air. Staying out of the heat helps animals conserve the water they get from the plants or animals they eat.

Who Are the "Hidden" Desert Animals?

DESERT HEDGEHOGS, found in Africa and the Middle East, escape the heat by staying in their burrows by day and hunting by night. One of the smallest species of hedgehog, they eat a varied diet, including insects, bird eggs, snakes, and scorpions.

GAMBEL'S QUAIL are ground-dwelling birds that live in the Sonoran, Mohave, and Chihuahuan Deserts. They prefer to walk or run rather than fly, but when frightened they burst into sudden, short flights. They live in large groups called "coveys," scratching for food under shrubs and cacti.

GERBILS are native to sandy areas of Africa, the Middle East, and Asia. They are nocturnal, taking advantage of cooler nights to search for food, which they often bring back to their burrows.

BLUE-TONGUED SKINKS, a type of lizard, bask in the hot Australian sun. When threatened, they stick out their large, blue tongues to scare away predators. And if caught, they bite off their tails to escape. Their tails will eventually grow back.

TARANTULAS are large, hairy spiders that live in warm areas around the world. South America has the greatest concentration. They live in underground burrows during the day, killing their prey at night with their venomous fangs.

HARRIS' HAWKS soar in groups high overhead in the Sonoran Desert to spot animals on the ground. Known as "wolves of the air," they use a cooperative hunting strategy—two or more hawks flush an animal from cover so that it may be captured by another hawk. Prey includes rabbits, ground squirrels, and rodents.

ELF OWLS are the world's smallest owl, about the size of a soda can. Abandoned woodpecker holes made in saguaro cacti in the Sonoran Desert provide safe places for elf owls to nest and raise their young. At night these tiny birds prey on arthropods, such as crickets, moths, and even scorpions.

CENTRAL ASIAN PIT VIPERS are venomous snakes that hunt primarily at night feeding on rodents, lizards, frogs, and insects. They open their mouths wide (180 degrees) to inject venom into their prey

PAINTED LADY BUTTERFLIES winter in the Sonoran Desert from November to early May. After a cool night in the desert, they warm up in the morning sun before flying off to sip nectar from flowers. They migrate north for the summer.

SPOTTED HYENAS can be found along the southern edge of the Sahara Desert and adjacent savannas. These carnivores are sometimes solitary scavengers, but will also hunt in packs for prey. The sound of their laughter is one of the most recognizable sounds of Africa.

About the Animals in the Story

Camels have pads of thick, leathery skin on their leg joints enabling them to *kneel* in the hot sand. There are two types of camels: the Dromedary, with one hump, and the Bactrian, with two humps. The Dromedary, also called the Arabian camel, is the one in this book. Well-adapted to desert life, camels have a third clear eyelid that protects their eyes from sandstorms. Camels can go without water for about a week and without food for several months. Their humps store fat, not water, and they also absorb heat. Camels usually have one baby called a **calf**.

Gila Monsters (pronounced HEE-luh) are one of the few poisonous lizards in the world. Native to the United States, they spend most of the day under cover or in burrows. Hunting at night, they *flick* their forked tongues to sense their prey (small mammals, birds, frogs, and other lizards) which they swallow whole. Because they store fat in their tails, they can go without food for months. A female lays an average of five eggs, then leaves. About four months later the **hatchlings** emerge and must survive on their own.

Meerkats are small mammals about the size of a squirrel. They dig underground burrows in the Kalahari Desert, where they live in small groups. They often use their long tails as a third leg to *stand* upright as they keep watch for predators. One meerkat acts as a lookout while the mob searches for food. If a predator is spotted, the guard lets out a shrill cry. Meerkats are primarily insectivores, but they will also eat lizards and snakes. They can even eat scorpions because they're immune to the scorpion's strong venom. They produce two to four **pups** a year.

Dingoes are medium-sized wild dogs that live in Australia. Able to survive in a variety of habitats, they are also found in Southeast Asia. Unlike dogs, they do not bark. But they sometimes howl like wolves. They're social animals that live in packs of about ten animals. Hunting at night, either alone or in a group, dingoes use their keen sense of smell to *sniff* for prey which includes rats, rabbits, birds, lizards, and even kangaroos. They will also eat fruits and plants. Dingoes have one litter of five to six **pups** a year.

Screaming Hairy Armadillos get their name from the squealing noise they make if they're threatened. Like all armadillos, much of this animal's body is covered with a thick armor, but they have more hair than other types of armadillos. Screaming hairy armadillos are native to the Monte Desert, just east of the Andes Mountains in South America. They like loose soil so they can *dig* burrows and escape predators. Once a year two **pups** are born in a litter. Often one is male and one is female.

Javelinas (pronounced hah-vuh-LEE-nuh) are also known as collared peccaries because the light hair around their necks can look like a collar. They live in family groups of ten or more in southwestern U.S. deserts, as well as Mexico, Central America, and northern Argentina. They communicate with each other with *snorts*, squeals, woofs, and by clicking their teeth. Mainly nocturnal herbivores, they eat a variety of plants, including the prickly pear cacti. They typically have two babies, called **reds** because of the color of their hair when young.

Desert Tortoises have lived in the Sonoran Desert for millions of years. They *hide* from predators by completely withdrawing their heads and limbs into their shells. Their strong forearms and sharp nails help them dig long burrows where they can escape the heat. They are herbivores, eating primarily wildflowers when in bloom, grasses, and cacti. A desert tortoise can go up to a year without drinking water. A female tortoise lays from one to fourteen eggs. Unlike the mother in the story, she leaves before the **hatchlings** come out of their shells, so they must survive on their own.

Gobi Jerboas (pronounced jer-BO-uh) are rodents that are adapted to living in the cold Gobi desert. Other species of jerboas are adapted for hot deserts. They always walk on their hind legs, rather than on all fours, using their extremely long tails for balance when running. They are most active at night, using their whiskers to feel their surroundings in the dark. With huge ears, they have excellent hearing. Jerboas can *jump* 10 feet (3 m) when being chased by a predator. Females have 2-6 **pups** in each litter and usually have 2-3 litters a year.

Roadrunners, also called Ground Cuckoos, are birds that run rather than fly. They can run at speeds of up to 15 miles (24 km) per hour in the Chihuahuan Desert. With two toes facing forward and two backwards, they make X-shaped tracks. Roadrunners are omnivores that feed on fruit, lizards, rodents, and insects. They even eat venomous rattlesnakes and scorpions. Females lay 3-8 white eggs in cup-like nests in mesquite bushes or cacti where the **chicks** will hatch. Roadrunners make *cooing* calls.

Fennec Foxes have enormous ears that help them *listen* for their prey from a long distance in the Sahara Desert. Their ears also help them stay cool by releasing excess heat. Another way they stay cool is to stay in their underground dens during the day. They hunt at night for small animals, insects, lizards, birds, and eggs. They can survive without access to water, getting what they need from their food. They live in groups of as many as ten and mark their territory with urine. A female gives birth to a litter of one to five **kits**.

From the Author

By the Numbers

As stated in "Fact or Fiction," the number of babies in the rhyme isn't necessarily the actual number of babies each animal has. The actual number of babies is explained in "About the Animals in the Story." Compare the number of fictional and factual babies to discover the similarities and differences. For example, the camel in the rhyme has one calf, and camels in the desert usually have just one calf – the number of baby camels is the same. The fennec fox in the rhyme has 10 kits, but fennec foxes in the desert have from one to five kits – the number of baby fennec foxes is different. You may use the comparisons to create addition or subtraction problems.

Act It Out

Using a paper plate and crayons or markers, have each child make a mask of one of desert animals in the story. Discuss the actions each animal does, such as kneel, sniff, hide, listen, and so on. Have children wear their masks while you read the story aloud. When you read the verse for their animal, have them act out the animal's action.

Fun with Words

Create a Word Wall to introduce new vocabulary words from the story, such as *thrive, crepuscular, mesquite, cacti, aridity, drought,* and *evaporation.* After reading the story, have children add other words to the wall that relate to a desert or animal. Children can use the words in a creative writing activity or in captions to pictures they draw.

Construct an Attribute Chart

After reading the story, construct an Attribute Chart. For young children, you may use a three-column chart, with category headings across the top, such as "Name of Desert," "Desert Animal," and "Baby Name." You may add more columns for older students, such as "Actions," "Foods" (omnivore, carnivore or herbivore), and "When Active" (nocturnal or diurnal).

A Closer Look at Deserts Around the World

Look at the map at the end of the story and ask children to name the continents where deserts are found. Which continent doesn't have a desert? Which desert in the story is a cold desert? Which deserts are in the United States? Have children make a pie graph showing that 20% of the land on Earth is desert. Older children can make bar graphs showing the size of each desert.

Design a Desert Animal

Refer to the illustrations and information provided under "Desert Facts," "Who are the 'Hidden' Animals," and "The Animals in the Story" to explain desert animal adaptations to children. Ask them to design a desert animal that uses at least one adaptation for living in the desert. Children may make a drawing of their animal, or you may provide various supplies and art materials to have them create a 3-D model. Have children draw or paint a desert mural on butcher paper to serve as a backdrop to display their creations.

Create a Cacti Garden

Because cacti come in a variety of shapes and sizes, they make an interesting indoor garden. Different types of cacti may be planted together in a shallow, unglazed terra cotta pot using a 50/50 mixture of coarse sand and houseplant potting soil. Water the cacti well when first planted. Once their roots are established, be careful not to overwater. The cacti will grow well in a location with a lot of light—a southern or southeastern exposure is ideal.

Discover More About Deserts

☀ Arizona-Sonora Desert Museum—Teacher resources including plant and animal facts. www.desertmuseum.org/kids/

☀ National Geographic Kids—Kid-friendly facts, photos, and videos. kids.nationalgeographic.com/explore/nature/habitats/desert/

☀ DesertUSA—Background information for parents and teachers. www.desertusa.com

For more activities, go to www.dawnpub.com and click on "Activities." Scroll to the cover of this book. You will find lesson plans aligned with Common Core and Next Generation Science Standards, along with reproducible bookmarks of the ten main animals in this book.

From the Illustrator

Each page of a book is unique. Every illustration must stand on its own, and it also needs to fit into the book as a whole. The author often gives me some indication as to what should be included in my illustration. In *Over on a Desert*, each animal is doing something. The dingo is sniffing, the armadillo is digging, and the jerboa is jumping.

Along with the action of each animal, many of these animals are active at a specific time of day.

The story says that the jerboas "often go out late," which told me I'd be drawing a night scene. It's always a challenge to draw a nighttime illustration because I want it to be obvious that it's dark out, yet it can't be so dark that you can't see the animals clearly. I have lots of papers that I use for my illustrations, but I often find I'm looking for something just a little different from what's in front of me. So I experiment to see how I can get what I want. For the jerboa, I used pastels to mute the papers to create a night scene.

Fennec foxes are also active at night, and I decided to create a scene at sunset. The kits are inside their den listening to the coming night sounds from the world outside. Because it's sunset, I could use warm colors that show night approaching, but it's not completely dark like the sky on the jerboa illustration. I think sunset works well as an ending of the day and also the ending of the book.

From the Book Designer

I have visited and loved deserts all over the world, and there is one special desert experience I want to share with you—a trip to the White Desert in Egypt. Our Bedouin guide drove us by jeep into a surreal landscape of deep-red sand and milk-white rock "sculptures" shaped like mushrooms and birds. Scattered among the white rocks were small black volcanic "flowers." Exquisite! We set up a simple camp in the sand with a pit for cooking dinner and cleared spaces for the long-haired camel blankets that would be our beds. Our guide made a wonderful meal for us of grilled chicken and vegetables, and I photographed the sunset. Night fell, and we were sitting around our campfire sharing stories. Suddenly I heard far away yip-yips and asked our guide what it was. He said they were the foxes, and he started yipping back. It was then that I looked off into the darkness and spotted the two

shiny eyes. We all got quiet, and up came a beautiful fennec fox. It sat down a couple of feet away from me, and I slowly moved my camera closer and turned off the flash even though it was night. I figured the flash would frighten our visitor. Our guide tossed the fox a little piece of chicken left over from our dinner. He then set out a cup of water for the fox, and that is when I took this picture lit only by our campfire. A magical night on the desert! You can see more of my images from the White Desert of Egypt at www.pattyarnold.com/whitedesert.html

Over on a Desert

Sung to the tune "Over in the Meadow"

Traditional Tune
Words by Marianne Berkes

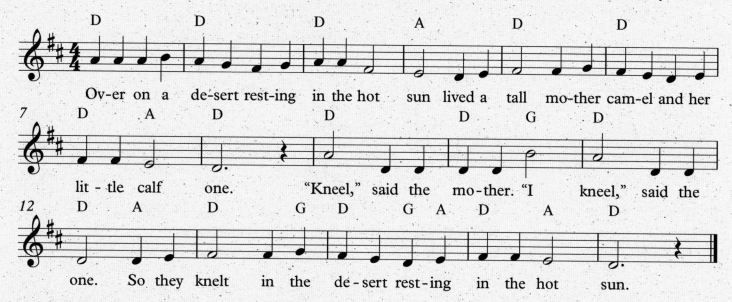

Ov-er on a de-sert rest-ing in the hot sun lived a tall mo-ther cam-el and her lit-tle calf one. "Kneel," said the mo-ther. "I kneel," said the one. So they knelt in the de-sert rest-ing in the hot sun.

2. Over on a desert
    Where the barrel cactus grew
    Lived a mother gila monster
    And her little hatchlings two.

    "Flick," said the mother.
    "We flick," said the two.
    So they flicked with their tongues
    Where the barrel cactus grew.

3. Over on a desert
    Near a camelthorn tree
    Lived a slender mother meerkat
    And her little pups three.

    "Stand" said the mother
    "We stand," said the three.
    So they stood and they watched
    Near a camelthorn tree.

4. Over on a desert
    On a hot, sandy floor
    Lived a wild mother dingo
    And her little pups four.

    "Sniff," said the mother.
    "We sniff," said the four.
    So they sniffed in a pack
    On a hot, sandy floor.

5. Over on a desert
    Where mesquite trees thrive
    Lived a mother armadillo
    And her little pups five.

    "Dig," said the mother.
    "We dig," said the five.
    So they dug with their claws
    Where mesquite trees thrive.

6. Over on a desert
    Eating cactus that pricks
    Lived a mother javelina
    And her little reds six.

    "Snort," said the mother.
    "We snort," said the six.
    So they grunted and they snorted
    Eating cactus that pricks.

7. Over on a desert
    Where saguaros reach to heaven
    Lived a mother desert tortoise
    And her little hatchlings seven.

    "Hide," said the mother.
    "We hide," said the seven.
    So they hid in their shells
    Where saguaros reach to heaven.

8. Over on a desert
    Where they often go out late
    Lived a shy mother jerboa
    And her little pups eight.

    "Jump," said the mother.
    "We jump," said the eight.
    So they jumped way up high
    Where they often go out late.

9. Over on a desert
    In the hot sunshine
    Lived a mother roadrunner
    And her little chicks nine.

    "Coo," said the mother.
    "We coo," said the nine.
    So they cooed as they ran
    In the hot sunshine.

10. Over on a desert
    In their underground den
    Lived a clever desert fox
    And his little kits ten.

    "Listen," said the father.
    "We listen," said the ten.
    As they heard the sound of laughing
    From their underground den.

MARIANNE BERKES has spent much of her life as a teacher, children's theater director, and children's librarian. She has put these experiences to good use as an author of over 20 entertaining and educational picture books that make learning relevant for young children. Her books are also inspired by her love of nature. She hopes to open kids' eyes to the magic found in our natural world. She is an energetic presenter at schools and literary conferences nationwide. Contact her at www.MarianneBerkes.com.

JILL DUBIN'S whimsical art has appeared in over 30 children's books. Her cut paper illustrations reflect her interest in combining color, pattern, and texture. She grew up in Yonkers, New York, and graduated from Pratt Institute. She lives with her family in Atlanta, Georgia, including two dogs that do very little but with great enthusiasm. Visit her at www.JillDubin.com

DEDICATIONS

To my friend and editor Carol Malnor——MB

To Marianne Berkes, your words are an inspiration for me and all who are touched by them.——JD

Book design and computer production by
Patty Arnold, *Menagerie Design & Publishing*

DAWN PUBLICATIONS

12402 Bitney Springs Road
Nevada City, CA 95959
530-274-7775
nature@dawnpub.com

Library of Congress Cataloging-in-Publication Data
Names: Berkes, Marianne Collins, author. | Dubin, Jill, illustrator.
Title: Over on a desert : somewhere in the world / by Marianne Berkes ; illustrated by Jill Dubin.
Description: Nevada City, CA : Dawn Publications, [2018] | Summary: A counting book in rhyme that presents various animals and their offspring that dwell in desert environments around the world, from a mother camel and "her little calf one" to a father fennec fox and "his little kits ten." Includes related facts and activities.
Identifiers: LCCN 2017043050| ISBN 9781584696292 (hardback) | ISBN 9781584696308 (pbk.)
Subjects: | CYAC: Stories in rhyme. | Desert animals--Fiction. | Animals--Infancy--Fiction. | Counting.
Classification: LCC PZ8.3.B4557 Owi 2018 | DDC [E]--dc23 LC record available at https://lccn.loc.gov/2017043050

Manufactured by Regent Publishing Services, Hong Kong
Printed July, 2018, in ShenZhen, Guangdong, China

10 9 8 7 6 5 4 3 2 1
First Edition

ALSO BY MARIANNE BERKES AND JILL DUBIN

Over in the Arctic: Where the Cold Winds Blow — This charming counting rhyme introduces creatures of the tundra.

Over in Australia: Amazing Animals Down Under — Australian animals are often unique, many with pouches for the babies. Such fun!

Over in the Forest: Come and Take a Peek — Follow the tracks of forest animals, but watch out for the skunk!

Over in a River: Flowing Out to the Sea — Beavers, manatees, and so many more animals help teach the geography of 10 great North American rivers.

Over on a Mountain: Somewhere in the World — Twenty different animals, ten great mountain ranges, and seven continents all in one story!

Over in the Grasslands: On an African Savanna — Come along on a safari! Through engaging rhyme you'll discover elephants, giraffes, meerkats, and more.

MORE BOOKS BY MARIANNE BERKES

Over in the Ocean: In a Coral Reef — With unique and outstanding style, this popular book portrays a vivid community of marine creatures.

Over in the Jungle: A Rainforest Rhyme — This book captures a rain forest teeming with remarkable animals.

Over on the Farm — Welcome to the farm, where pigs roll, goats nibble, horses gallop, hens peck, and turkeys strut! Count, clap, and sing along.

Going Around the Sun: Some Planetary Fun — Earth is part of a fascinating "family" of planets. Here's a glimpse of the "neighborhood."

Going Home: The Mystery of Animal Migration — Many animals migrate "home," often over great distances. A solid introduction to the phenomenon of migration.

Seashells by the Seashore — Kids discover, identify, and count twelve beautiful shells to give Grandma for her birthday.

The Swamp Where Gator Hides — Still as a log, only his watchful eyes can be seen. But when gator moves, he really moves!

What's in the Garden? — Good food doesn't begin on a store shelf in a box. It comes from a garden bursting with life!

Baby On Board — Kids will be fascinated by all of the clever ways animal parents carry their young.

MAY WE ALSO RECOMMEND . . .

Tall Tall Tree—Take a peek at some of the animals that make their home in a tall, tall tree—a magnificent coast redwood. Rhyming verses and a 1-10 counting scheme made this a real page-turner.

Daytime Nighttime, All Through the Year—Delightful rhymes depict two animals for each month, one active during the day and one busy at night. See all the action!

Octopus Escapes Again!—Swim along with Octopus as she searches for food. Will she eat or be eaten? She outwits dangerous enemies by using a dazzling display of defenses.

Paddle, Perch, Climb: Bird feet Are Neat—Become a bird detective as you meet the feet that help birds eat—so many different shapes, sizes, and ways to use them. It's time for lunch!

E-I-E-I-O Book Series—Follow the adventures of young Jo, granddaughter of Old MacDonald, as she discovers the delights of the pond, woods, and garden on Old MacDonald's farm in *Jo MacDonald Saw a Pond, Jo MacDonald Hiked in the Woods,* and *Jo MacDonald Had a Garden.*

Dawn Publications is dedicated to inspiring in children a deeper understanding and appreciation for all life on Earth. You can browse through our titles, download resources for teachers, and order at www.dawnpub.com or call 800-545-7475.